SCROOGE ME HARD

PARANORMAL DATING AGENCY 9.5

NEW YORK TIMES and USA TODAY
BESTSELLING AUTHOR
MILLY TAIDEN

This book is a work of fiction. The names, characters, places, and incidents are fictitious or have been used fictitiously, and are not to be construed as real in any way. Any resemblance to persons, living or dead, actual events, locales, or organizations is entirely coincidental.

Published By
Latin Goddess Press
New York, NY 10456
http://millytaiden.com
Scrooge Me Hard
Copyright © 2015 & 2016 by Milly Taiden
Edited by Tina Winograd
Cover by Willsin Rowe
All Rights Are Reserved. No part of this book may be used or reproduced in any manner whatsoever without written permission, except in the case of brief quotations embodied in critical articles and reviews.
Property of Milly Taiden 2015 2016

❀ Created with Vellum

—For My Readers

Enjoy this sexy holiday romance of second chance love.

Aurelis Fuentes wants one thing: children. She'd also like people to stop complaining about not enough frosting on her cupcakes, but that's another story. When her scrooge of an ex comes back into her life, she's not sure what to think.

Reed Stone wants one thing: his mate back. He made a mistake, but he's a changed man. In the spirit of Christmas, he's hoping she takes a chance and forgives him or at least allows him to explain without throwing things at him.

Gerri Wilder is at it again, only this time she's got the help of some of our previous couples. Catch up with Tally, Nita, Maya, Alyssa and their men while they try to help Auri and Reed find their way back to each other. This is one holiday they won't soon forget.

CHAPTER ONE

Gerri smiled at the decorations around the city. She loved the holidays. She'd recently gotten back from Aurora and managed to hire a new assistant. Cassie was doing a great job at setting up Gerri's office into a much more manageable work area. Now all Gerri needed was rest.

On her way home, she passed a gaggle of kids tossing snowballs back and forth. A particular young one sitting away from the others caught her eye. The little boy's big blue eyes stared at her with open curiosity. He reminded her of a mini Reed Stone. Did he have a child she hadn't met?

She laughed to herself. According to what she

knew of Reed, him having a child was close to an ice cube's chance in hell.

Reed had been one of the children her husband had mentored when he'd been alive. He'd taught him how to run a business and eventually start one from scratch. She hadn't seen Reed in too long. All her recent travels had kept her from catching up with him.

"Hello, handsome fellow," she said to the young child. "What's your name?"

"Gavin," he said, offering a mitten-covered hand to shake. "How are you?"

Oh, my. She grabbed his little hand and shook. "Why aren't you a little gentleman? I'm doing very good, now that you've asked, sir. Tell me something, Gavin, are you all alone or is one of the older boys your brother?"

He shook his head. "My brother is in the bakery."

She glanced over her shoulder at Aurelis's bakery. The curvaceous baker had amazing hands when it came to food. It was a wonder the place wasn't continuously packed. She'd always felt there was more than met the eye with the baker. Her scent was different; there was more shifter than human in her.

Gerri frowned at the couple arguing inside the bakery. Clearly Aurelis was having a hard time with a client. She turned back to Gavin with a frown. "Would you like a cookie, Gavin?"

He nodded, eyes and smile wide. Gerri took the boy by his hand and pushed the bakery door open, watching the quarreling adults clam up and turn to look at her.

Aurelis's normally dark brown eyes showed a hint of gold. Interesting.

The man still had his back to her, but a good whiff, and Gerri was smiling.

"Reed?"

He turned, his bright golden eyes caught her by surprise. Boy, he was quite angry. His animal was ready to tear into his very expensive looking suit and coat and make himself known.

"Gerri?" His words were low and gruff with his animal. He marched over and embraced Gerri in a hug. "It's been so long."

Too long. Where the hell had she been when Reed had grown so damn handsome. She pulled back, her gaze gliding back and forth between Reed and Aurelis. "You look amazing, Reed."

She racked her brain for the last time she'd seen him. It was almost ten years. Lord, where did time go? At her charity function--that's where she'd seen him last. She held him at arm's length and took in all of the big wolf she'd once known as a boy as young as Gavin. Remembering the child, her eyes roamed the room for a boy close to Gavin's age. No one else was in the store. Odd.

"My cookie?" Gavin asked, bringing all eyes to him.

Aurelis rushed behind the counter and picked two chocolate chip that smelled heavenly. Cookies wrapped in a napkin, she darted around and bent down to hand Gavin his dessert. "Here you go, baby."

"It's good to see you, Gerri," Aurelis said. She was pissed. Gerri could always tell when the Latina was angry because her accent became thicker. Usually it was when she was overrun with clients who demanded to be served before others, like they had some special privilege.

Gerri's mind kicked into overdrive. Could Gavin be Reed's little brother? Thirty years his senior?

"We should go," Reed told Gavin. The child didn't appear concerned with anything but his treats. Reed glanced at Gerri and gave her a warm smile. "I'll give you a call this week so we can have dinner. It's been too long."

She nodded. "You're right. I can't believe I've been so busy I hadn't noticed we haven't seen each other."

He barked a laugh that made his ocean-blue eyes bright with mirth. "You've been busy matchmaking everyone in this city…and beyond."

Gerri winked. "Careful, before I set my sights on you."

She didn't miss the frown on Aurelis's face along with the soft growl coming from the baker or the way he glanced at Aurelis. That little smirk could get a man killed.

"Maybe we should talk about it." He grinned.

Aurelis cleared her throat. "What can I do for you, Gerri?"

"Just a second, Aurelis." She turned to Gavin and shook his hand. "Thank you for escorting me inside the bakery."

He nodded. "You're welcome."

"Would you like to come to a big party at a mansion a friend of mine owns?" she asked the boy.

His eyes widened, then he glanced at Reed. "What kind of party?"

"It's a huge holiday event. For children and adults. Each one has their own side of the mansion." She squatted to Gavin's height. "The best part? There will be tons of desserts and presents." She bit her lip to keep from laughing at how wide the boy's eyes got. "And even Santa."

He gasped. "Santa?"

She nodded solemnly. "Yes. You should come. In fact, you should make Reed bring you. It will be the biggest bash of this holiday season."

Gavin glanced up at Reed with puppy dog eyes and Gerri knew the kid had him in the palm of his hand. "Can we go to the dash, Reed? Please?"

She saw the way Reed's shoulders dropped enough to let her know the adorable kid had won. Good going, Gavin, even though he didn't say the right word.

"I'll think about it. We should go before your stepmother starts wondering where you are."

Reed stared at Aurelis for a silent moment before following Gavin. That look said more than any words.

CHAPTER TWO

Aurelis hadn't seen Reed in almost five years. He'd been busy, traveling. At least, that's what he said. She told herself she didn't care, but she did. Oh, she did. So much so, she followed up on everything about him in the business news. Stone Jewelry had made quite a name for itself. All thanks to him. Her mate.

She found it funny that most people didn't realize she was mated. She'd done a damn good job of keeping her business to herself. Not to mention she left Reed years ago after a bitter argument over having children. Children and Christmas. The two things he'd been against from the very beginning.

When Reed walked into her bakery, holding Gavin's little hand, she'd almost had a heart attack. Reed had been quick to send Gavin out to play in the snow. The shocked then murderous look she must've had probably scared both of them a little.

Once Gavin was out the door, she proceeded to throw the first thing she could, which was a short stack of paper coffee cups. He'd raised his hands and said the magic words before she could let loose and make a pan of brownies fly his way. *"He's my brother, Auri. He's not my son."*

Things calmed some after that, but she was still angry he'd come into her bakery after five years of ignoring her.

"So," Gerri lifted her brows. "You and Reed, huh?"

Auri, her name with family and friends, glanced at the display case of decadent cakes and cookies amongst other pastries, and pulled out a chocolate cake. Her personal favorite. Auri placed a piece on an elegant white porcelain plate. Then she put a few of Gerri's beloved chocolate chip and macadamia nut cookies on another plate and skimmed around the counter. She stopped by one of the tables decorated with red tablecloths and green napkins.

"Come, sit down, Gerri," she replied. "If you're going to interrogate me then let me at least have some cake."

Gerri hurried around the counter, filled two coffee cups with freshly brewed hot chocolate and sat across from her with a sigh.

"Honey, I'm not going to interrogate you." Gerri picked up a cookie and chewed slowly. "If you are not up to talking, I understand. But I won't stop you."

She licked her lips after her first bite of cake. This recipe got her into starting her own business. She had taken the plunge because Reed had raved about it, and told her he believed she could be successful.

"It's fine. I've hidden behind denial long enough. Figures you'd know him."

"Sweetheart, I don't just know Reed," Gerri told her with authority. "I spent more time with him and Noah than any other teenagers."

Now there was something Auri hadn't expected. Maybe Gerri had insight into why Reed had been so against having children and hated the holidays.

"We weren't together long," she admitted. It was true. She'd been with Reed for a matter of weeks. A whirlwind relationship. Like being on an adrenaline high. He'd gotten into her system and she'd been unable to get him out.

Gerri nodded sympathetically. "All you need is one day. A shifter man will get in your blood. He'll cause you to question the things you promised yourself you didn't need and then you'll crave them."

Auri met Gerri's gaze. She'd been reading her mind. She had to. How in the world did she know that?

All her life, Auri had known she wanted to have kids. Lots of kids. She'd been raised in a large extended family, but was an only child. Having her aunts, cousins, and everyone around when her parents died had sealed the idea in her mind. After numerous relationships had gone nowhere, she met Reed outside a diner she worked at.

"I've come to know you the past few years, and I can't imagine someone with your carefree personality being in a relationship with Reed."

Auri snorted. "Neither could I, after a while."

"So how did that come about?"

"It was really funny, actually. He hit me with his car."

"What?" Gerri gasped.

"Not hurting me. It was pouring outside, and I was running across the street to catch a bus when he came out of nowhere."

"Oh, my god. He really hit you?" Gerri blinked.

"No, he stopped in time, but I fell from the shock of him being so close. It scared the shit out of me." She laughed. "He got out of his car, angry at first that I'd run into the street without looking. Then he got really quiet, picked me up in his arms and took me home."

Gerri's surprise turned to a wide grin. "Ah, he realized you were his mate."

"Something like that." She sipped her hot chocolate while reminiscing. When she'd first seen Reed, he'd been so big and powerful. He'd scared her a little. Not because she felt she couldn't handle him, but because he'd shown so much interest in her. She'd fallen head over heels so fast, she didn't know how it happened. To this day, the man had the ability to give her butterflies in her belly with a single hot look.

"So what happened? What went wrong?"

Auri shrugged and drank more chocolate. "He didn't want kids." She licked the cream off her lips.

"And he hated the holidays. I was so excited to have him come over and meet my family, to share our traditions." She shook her head. "He wasn't interested. Said he hated Christmas, and it wasn't up for debate."

"Ouch." Gerri patted Auri's hand. "So what's he doing here now?"

She rolled her eyes. "Something about me not signing the divorce papers when they sent them."

Gerri's eyes went wide. "Wait, you're married?"

A flush of heat crept over her cheeks. "Yes. It was a crazy few weeks."

"And he really wants a divorce?" The shock in Gerri's words surprised her. Why wouldn't he? They'd been separated for years.

"He said we needed to talk. That we had unfinished business." She took a bite of cake. "I assume that's what he wants. To finalize the divorce."

"Why didn't you sign the papers?"

"I never got them." Aurelis pushed a stray strand of dark hair behind her ear. "I really thought he'd come to his senses, but right after that I started my business and things just took off. For the first few years, I was so involved in working all the time and building my bakery that I just didn't think about him." She pressed her lips together. "I tried hard not to, anyway."

"Maybe he's changed?" There was a note of hope in Gerri's voice.

"I don't know. I don't really know if I care at this point. He could have come back at any time, but he chose to travel and stay away." She glanced down at her cake. "If that isn't enough to let me know I'm not important, then I don't know what is."

"I understand your hesitation. This is unexpected. What you need right now is more work," Gerri grinned. "A big project."

Auri laughed at the way Gerri waggled her brows. "Oh, yes. Work is so sexy."

"I happen to think chocolate is very sexy." Gerri laughed. "Anyway, what I want is for you to host and cater my Christmas party this year."

"Isn't it like a few days away?" Auri's shock made her voice grow high pitched. "Only a few days?"

Gerri nodded. "I've been traveling. You know how it is. You'll have full rein of the food."

"You have people at that mansion that can cook for you. Why me?"

Gerri smiled. "I like you. This would get your name out there even more."

She was right. Auri needed the job. It could bring in potential new clients and even though she didn't need a lot of money to live on, growing her business was her priority.

"Okay, Gerri. I'm all yours."

CHAPTER THREE

Reed Stone watched Gavin playing with the giant building blocks he'd brought him. His *way* younger little brother. With wheat blond hair and bright blue eyes, the four-year-old was the spitting image of Reed and his father Charles. Back when Charles had been able to do things. Now, the wolf-shifter was bed bound, dying.

"Reed," Gavin said glancing up from his blocks. "Play with me."

He sat with his brother, over thirty years younger than him and easily able to pass for his son. Except that Reed had no kids. And until he'd met Gavin, he'd had no intention of having any children.

Gavin played by the giant Christmas tree his stepmother had ordered and placed in the center of her sitting room. Unlike the past wives, who only cared about shopping, his father's current wife had done a great job of getting to know the help around the mansion. She cared about them and the upkeep of their massive home, which was pretty hard considering the size of the house.

Built in the center of twenty acres of forest, the mansion had its own driveway and dual entry gates. Not that Charles ever cared about trespassers in the past. Recently, though, with Reed traveling the need to ensure the family's safety had made the security necessary.

The house was modern in style with some interesting architectural designs. It had a lot of glass, which allowed for the feel of the outdoors being brought inside. The furniture and décor were all the latest trend, but minimalist in style to keep from needing extensive amounts of cleaners running around the house.

His father's wife had taken the sitting room and turned it into a play area for Gavin, something Reed knew none of Charles' ex-wives would have ever done. Though it still screamed money with some antique pieces passed from generation to generation. Not to mention the Macassar Ebony floors in most of the ten bedrooms. It featured white marble floors and an antique dual circular staircase his mother had designed and shipped from France, with intricate carvings of running wolves by a top Parisian artist.

The main ballroom was now used to host family gatherings and friendly dinners rather than the expensive balls and parties Charles's exes had all deemed the most important thing to do. The tennis and basketball courts had been opened to local youth groups, cutting the area off from the rest of the house. Reed had built a secondary building by the courts with showers and lockers for the kids.

The sound of the door chime made him glance up to catch the housekeeper heading past the sitting room to open it. She returned moments later with Gerri Wilder behind her.

"Reed," Gerri grinned. "You know I couldn't just forget about what happened last night."

He'd figured that. Gerri wasn't one of those people. In fact, once he'd seen her at Auri's bakery, he'd been hoping she'd show up at the house. Ideally his penthouse, but he guessed she must have tried him here first.

"I didn't expect you would, Gerri," he said, getting up.

"Hello, little Gavin. How are you today?" Gerri asked and offered a hand to his brother.

"Good. Playing."

"I see that." Gerri laughed. "Looks like you have a city under construction."

Reed asked the housekeeper to find Gavin's stepmother. Unlike Gavin's birth mother, she'd want to spend time with the child, playing and caring for him.

"Would you like some tea?" He remembered when he was a kid, Gerri made tea as a way to get him to talk to her. She'd sit and have him drink and stare at him. For one hour every day, he'd have to sit there and if he didn't want to talk about anything, she was fine with it, but he had to remain there anyway. His not talking didn't stop her from telling him about her life with her husband. Or her wish for children and never having any.

She nodded and followed him into the sitting room. "You know," she said, "I never thought I'd see the day you would find a woman. I've matched so many couples, but you went and found yours all on your own."

He picked up a phone and called the kitchen for tea. Then he turned to Gerri. "I also managed to get her to leave me and not approach her for enough time that she now wants nothing to do with me."

"Why didn't you tell her?" Gerri asked. "About the holiday season. Christmas. Gifts. The whole shebang."

He didn't feel he knew her well enough during the first few days. Once he married and mated her, he'd been so consumed with looking further into the future that he didn't want to discuss the past. *His* past, at that.

"It didn't feel important enough to talk about."

The tea arrived and gave him a moment before Gerri replied as she served her own tea.

"Reed, you know I love you," she told him. "But get your head out of your ass."

He wasn't surprised by her words. That was Gerri. She spoke her mind and told it as she saw it. Right now he was in agreement. He should have discussed his issues with Auri and maybe then she'd have understood. At least the holiday thing. "I don't know. She seemed set on wanting children right away."

Gerri took a sip of the hot liquid and sighed.

"This is good tea. Maybe the years we've been apart have made you forget how to use your brain."

"Why?"

"After all the time you spent on my couch like I was your therapist, you are telling me that you couldn't figure out you are worth all the love a woman, your mate, is willing to give. That includes children. They can give you love, too."

He'd learned that recently with Gavin. His little brother didn't ask for anything and openly loved Reed. He spent so much time with Reed it was as if he were his father instead of Charles.

"I know, now."

Gerri nodded. "So you've come to your senses and want her back."

He did. Not that he'd ever not wanted her. He just thought it best to let her go while he figured out the problems his father had gotten himself into with Gavin's mother. The time had dragged. His father re-married for the fifth time. Then his father got sick. The company needed Reed. Running two businesses took a toll on him.

"What do you want to hear? I never stopped loving Auri. Not a single moment. She's been present in my mind for the past five years."

Gerri leaned back in her seat and met his gaze

with her own serious one. "That's a long time to wait to go after a woman. One you say you love."

"I know. Life got in the way. A lot of things happened. I couldn't bring these problems to her when I didn't know what the outcome would be."

"It's horrible that you felt you had to deal with everything alone." She glanced down at her hands and then back at him. He saw a sad look in her eyes. "I tried to teach you I was there for you, Reed."

"You did teach me. You were there when nobody else was."

That was the ultimate truth. Gerri had been more of a mother than any of his father's ex-wives. Hell, she'd been more of a mother and a father than his own father. He'd been too busy looking for the next ex-Mrs. Stone to worry about what his son was feeling or doing.

"Don't worry," Gerri said, her eyes alive with excitement. "I have a plan that will right whatever is wrong with you and your mate."

"You do?" Great. His ideas weren't working out exactly like he'd planned. Showing up at her place of business and telling her they were still married therefore she was still his didn't have the effect he'd expected. He'd been lucky the paper coffee cups she'd thrown at him had been empty. That, and he had really good reflexes.

"Oh, I do. You'll have Aurelis back before you know it. Just don't mess it up, Reed. I love you, but I will hurt you if you do something to push her away again."

That was one mistake he didn't plan on making a second time.

CHAPTER FOUR

Auri glanced at the pile of clothing on her bed. She shouldn't be worried. It was just a party. A big, fucking party that could make or break her business. So what that she wasn't hurting for money, she wanted to see her desserts everywhere. Her business was her passion since her personal life tanked.

Her doorbell rang and she rushed over to open the door.

"Big cousin is here to help. I so got this." Violet marched inside with purpose, straight to Auri's bedroom where the dress explosion had happened.

"It's under control," Auri lied. She winced when she walked into her bedroom, getting a good look at the dresses strewn about the room.

Violet raised dark brows and stared at her. "If this is having it under control, I'd hate to see you letting it all go crazy."

She smiled at Violet and started rummaging through dresses again. "This is awful. It's not even about me. My desserts are making a statement tonight. The cookies, cakes, brownies, flans. You name it and I'm pretty sure I made it."

"Holiday themed?" Violet sighed. "I love Christmas. I love the lights. The sounds. The food."

"Yeah, so do I. That's why I'm so big, remember?"

Violet picked up a brown dress and made a face like she'd sucked on a lemon. "You're curvy, prima. We all are. It's just our bodies. I like to eat; I won't deny it. You like it too. That doesn't make us bad people, just fluffy girls."

"Real fluffy girls." Auri laughed. She was okay with that most of the time. It was days like today when she needed to make an impression on people and didn't know what to wear. She wanted to look professional, pretty, and not look ridiculous. "I've looked through everything, Violet. I got nothing and I have to get ready soon or I won't be there for the start of the party."

Violet shot to her feet and searched the

remaining clothes in the closet. She pulled out a plastic covered dress on a hanger. "What about this one?"

"No." The answer was immediate. That was the last dress she'd wear.

"But it's perfect," Violet said glancing at the gold dress with emerald green sash. "This is the dress. It's Christmasy and it's the type of cut that will flatter your curves."

Dammit. Why had she kept that dress? She didn't know. Nostalgia. Love. Wishing one day she'd get a chance to hit Reed in the face with it? She hadn't expected to wear it again.

"I can't wear that dress, Violet," she said quietly.

"Nonsense," Violet said. She pulled the dress out of the plastic casing and handed it to Auri with a firm stare. "Put it on. Whatever this dress meant, it doesn't hold that power, anymore. Give it new meaning."

She was right. Why was she letting the memory of her Christmas wedding influence her decision now, years later? She took it and went into the bathroom to change.

Once dressed, she came out and glanced in the full-body mirror in her bedroom.

"You look beautiful, Auri."

She'd bought that dress for one reason: she felt so pretty in it. It was a strapless gown in sheer gold chiffon threaded with shiny green line along the edge of the bottom. The green sash brocade added texture and matched beautifully with the silver pin covered in bling.

"Thanks," she choked the word out. Unlike the last time she wore the dress, she wasn't wearing her hair up on the side entwined with bits of red holly. This time, she chose to leave it loose, curling down her back. "I guess it's now or never."

Never sounded good, but now was the time to get on with growing her business. Besides, she highly doubted Reed would show up. He had been traveling the previous day, according to the news-paper. No way he'd come back just to go to a party. Not a Christmas party. Not when he hated the holiday.

CHAPTER FIVE

Reed ushered his father's current wife, Rosemary, and Gavin into the children's side of the event. Their part of the mansion had been decorated as a winter wonderland dream. Massive candy canes and fluffy snow clouds covered the space where the kids played. There were big snowmen in every corner of the room. Stars hung from the tall ceilings, making it look like they were really outside.

He watched Gavin head straight for a small table set up for children to make their own ornaments. Someone had an instant film camera and pasting the kids' photos on their ornaments then putting them on the big tree next to Santa's seat. The employees were dressed as elves giving out drinks. Labeled with the child's name, the cups looked like miniature Christmas trees with straws.

Off to the side were rows of finger foods for the children. Everything from fruit designs in Christmas colors, to desserts, cookies and punch. It was the ultimate feast.

Every time a child walked in, an employee placed a bracelet around their wrist with any food allergy comments. Those standing by the food lines ensured the children didn't eat anything that could make them sick. Gerri had truly done an outstanding job.

He watched his father's wife, Rosemary, sit next to Gavin, doing what she did best, pay attention to the child. Gavin had a rough start in life, but he had the best mother he could wish for now. Rosemary had taken care of him like he was her own. For once, Charles had done something right by one of his children and suckered in a woman who cared.

Gavin turned as if sensing Reed watching him and waved him goodbye. That was his cue. He headed for the other side of the mansion where adults mingled. Unlike the children's candy cane wonderland filled with toys and giant nutcrackers, the adult side was elegant and understated. Decorations were white snowflakes.

Crystal snowflakes and iridescent ornaments appeared to float from the ceiling. There were big silver ornaments along the sides, which upon further inspection, were seats.

Gerri had brought the outdoors inside this room as well. Centerpieces consisted of mini trees painted white with hanging crystals in the shape of snowballs. Tables had a satin white cloth and a sheer covering that gave a glistening shimmer. He was impressed.

"How do you like it?" Gerri asked, walking up to his side.

"It's nice. You really outdid yourself." He noticed the employees were also dressed as elves but instead of the green and red costumes as the children's side, these wore all white to blend in with the décor.

"Thanks. Aurelis did an amazing job with the food. She partnered with the chef, and between the two, they made an amazing menu."

He took a flute of champagne handed to him by one of the employees and turned to face Gerri. She wore her blond hair in a twist with a white ivy leaf holding her hairdo in place. She'd chosen a red dress that made her stand out from everyone wearing the usual dressy black or darker colors.

"You look great," he said and kissed her cheek.

"You're not so bad yourself." She patted his tux at the chest. "Now, your mate is about to head over to the kitchens so why don't you go say hello."

He grinned and nodded. "Always the matchmaker."

She raised a brow. "If I didn't help you, it would be painful to watch you try to convince her you are what she needs."

He laughed as he walked away, ready to do anything, and everything, to get Auri back. He caught sight of her by the dessert table. She wore the dress he married her in Christmas Eve five years ago. She looked as beautiful now as she did then. The dress outlined every big, delicious curve without showing off.

He remembered how excited she'd been to wear it the first time. Her gorgeous brown skin shimmered in the fabric, her face almost glowing with happiness. Her long, dark hair hung in curls down her back. He also remembered taking her out of it. Nearly tearing it off until she asked him not to because she wanted to keep the dress as a memory of the best day of her life. He doubted she saw it that way any longer. He needed her alone.

A quick glance around and he realized there were just too many people around, watching everything and everyone. This wasn't going to work. There was a lot she didn't know and he was ready to talk to her. He only hoped she was ready to listen.

Auri turned to find Gerri standing behind her.

"Gerri, hi. Every time I see you, you're surrounded by your guests. Big and small." She laughed.

Gerri grinned. "Hello. You look beautiful in that dress."

She fidgeted and shifted from foot to foot. "Thanks. I wasn't sure what to wear so this was it. How are you liking the party?"

"Oh, darling," Gerri patted her arm, "it's fantastic. You did a fabulous job."

"Me?" She shook her head. "All I did was make dessert. Your decorators, party planners, and chef deserve the credit for this."

The place looked amazing. Auri loved the holidays. It reminded her of family and being with loved ones. Gatherings where everyone played games, talked, and spent time together. That was what her family did. When Reed had refused to partake in the holidays with her, he'd broken her heart.

The worst part was that he didn't want to explain why. She might have been able to work around his problem, if she understood, but he'd been adamantly silent to why.

When the subject of children came around, his refusal was like a slap in the face. She might love him. Had fallen in love in an instant, but she wasn't staying in a dead-end relationship. Not even if it meant living alone for the rest of her life because no man measured up to him. No one made her feel the way he did.

"Are you looking for someone?" Gerri asked catching her glancing around the ballroom to make sure Reed hadn't shown up when she wasn't looking.

"What?" She met Gerri's humor-filled gaze and shook her head. She was glad her skin was dark enough or Gerri would notice the flush of heat crowding her cheeks.

Gerri placed the flute of her champagne on a table. Too close to the edge. The flute fell and filled the surrounding area with the sound of crystal breaking. Not many noticed. There was a band playing and most guests were on the dance floor.

"Let me get that," Auri said, instinctively pushing Gerri back so she wouldn't get cut. "I am pretty sure I saw a broom not more than a few moments ago."

"It's in the hallway closet, dear," Gerri said and pointed down a hall.

"I'll be right back. Don't let anyone around here."

Gerri nodded with a smile and winked. "I will stand guard."

Auri rushed down the hallway, opening door after door until she found a big closet filled with cleaning supplies. She glanced around, searching for the dust pan and broom. Suddenly, the door closed behind her. She whirled around to face Reed.

"What are you doing here?" Her voice came out breathless, husky.

He glanced at her face for a long moment, his eyes bright with his animal. His gaze moved down, focusing on her breasts as they rose and fell with each of her breaths. Then he went further down until he got to her feet and moved back up to her face. She'd never felt so naked with clothes on.

"You look beautiful."

She tried to get past him, but he flipped them around to put her back against the locked door and he pressed against her.

"Reed. Let me go."

"No."

She widened her eyes and growled. She'd been ignoring her wolf, wishing it would shut up about her desire for her mate. Sheer will had kept her sane through the years he'd ignored her. Forgotten her.

"You can't just show up and think we're going to pick up where we left off," she hissed, tugging at the hold he had on her wrists. "It doesn't work like that."

He pressed farther into her, pushing his erection on the folds of her dress. Lord, he felt so good. She missed him so much. Her need for him wasn't one she could ever get rid of. It was something she'd learned to live without.

"I know that," he growled softly. "I'm sorry."

"Sorry isn't good enough," she argued. "I had expectations for our relationship. I told you what they were and you decided not to tell me you disagreed until after we were married, mated, and my heart was on the line."

His brows drew down in a fierce scowl. "Don't kid yourself, babe. Your heart was on the line from the very first moment we saw each other."

"I don't give a shit!" She glared at him with all the pain and anger she'd suffered. "You don't get to come back and act like the past five years didn't happen. Fuck you, Reed. Now let me go."

"No." He didn't sweeten the words or even bother apologizing. Not that it would have helped. At least, she told herself that. No. Instead, he lowered his head and took her lips with his. He plunged his tongue into her mouth, savoring and devouring like he'd been dying for a taste of something denied to him.

She tried to fight it, fight him, but it was useless. Her body betrayed her when it came to him. She loved the man. She never stopped and never would. But that didn't mean she'd allow him to make a fool of her. She'd take his kiss. Lord, would she take it. She'd missed his touch so much. The feel of his lips brushing over hers, owning and demanding her acquiescence.

Her body ached for his touch. She held out as

long as she could, but the more she tried to act like he wasn't lighting flames in her soul, the more he pushed. He drove deeper with his tongue, rubbing and caressing hers. She moaned and gave up, giving back to the kiss as much as he gave.

He massaged her wrists against the door, pressing against her and rocking his hips so she'd feel more of his hardness.

He pulled back, groaning and raining kisses over her jaw and chest. "Tell me you didn't miss me, this, us. Tell me."

The sound of his words, hoarse, rough and hungry drove her own animal insane. She didn't get a chance to reply, his mouth was on her chest, licking at the seam of her dress and tugging down the neckline with his teeth. She pressed her head against the unforgiving wood of the door and shut her eyes. This had to stop. It was maddening. She wasn't his anymore. Who the fuck was she kidding? She'd always be his.

A low whimper escaped her throat as his teeth yanked down the material of her dress and her breasts popped up and out. He struck fast, latching on to her nipple and sucking deep and hard.

"Oh, god!" Her knees buckled from how good it

felt. Pleasure zigzagged from her nipples to her pussy, making her clit throb.

"Fuck!" He bit down on her nipple, making her squirm. "You taste like heaven and smell like the best dessert." He licked between her tits, curling his tongue in circles over the valley of her breasts. "I can't wait to get a taste of your cream."

A movement of the door knob shoved her out of the sex-hazed moment. She wiggled her body away from him.

"Stop, Reed, stop," she hissed.

He did. He met her gaze with his much more possessive golden one and growled low. "We need to talk. There are things I must tell you."

"Let go of my hands," she ordered.

He brought her arms down from the door and she fixed her dress, pushing her breasts into the built in bra. "We have nothing to talk about other than our divorce. I never got those papers." She ran shaky fingers through her hair. "Have your lawyer send them again. I'll happily sign them."

She turned the knob but he held the door in place. "I don't want a divorce."

With a deep breath, she glanced at him. "Why not?"

"I want you. We belong together."

She lifted her lips in a small, bitter smile. "You should have thought of that when you decided I was at the bottom of your priority list and you wouldn't speak to me until it was convenient. And since five years later is convenient for you, it's no longer convenient for me."

She turned the knob again and opened the door.

"This isn't over, Auri. We have things to talk about," he growled.

She marched away, not once looking back. Her stomach twisted in knots and nausea rolled up her throat. She needed a breath of fresh air or she'd lose her mind in the middle of the damn party.

Reed headed for one of the libraries, away from the happy couples dancing the night away. He was frustrated and didn't know what to do to control his wolf. The animal wanted his mate. He'd been denied far too long. There was no making him wait any longer.

When he entered the reading room, he found a group of men sitting around talking and drinking. He knew at least one of them from childhood.

"Noah?" Noah Wright was a friend from youth who'd grown up to be a big time video game designer and developer. They hadn't seen each other in a few years but they still kept in touch.

Noah raised a glass filled with amber liquid and

motioned him inside. "Come on in, Reed. Long time, no see."

Two guys played a video game on a massive eighty-inch screen while the others stood back and watched, all with either a beer or whiskey tumbler in hand. The men had removed their tux jackets and sat around casually.

"What are you guys doing?" Reed asked.

Noah pointed to the two guys on the couch, game controllers in their hands. "Theron and Connor are trying out my next game."

The screen image paused and both men turned to greet Reed.

"Hey, I'm Connor and this is Theron. And Noah's new game is fucking amazing. Wait 'til you try it."

He waved at the two men and turned to the other two guys talking. One wore glasses and the other didn't appear happy. "Hey," the glasses guy said. "I'm Ky, and this is Gray. You look like you could use a drink." He headed for a panel that opened into a fridge. "We have beer, wine, whiskey, and soft drinks."

"Beer, please," he said.

Ky handed him a brew and motioned him over. "Come on, bro. Tell us your troubles."

Reed laughed. "Is this a support group?"

The game was paused again and Theron and Connor nodded over their shoulders. Connor grinned. "When you're mated to very difficult women, you need a support group."

"Where the hell have you all been all my life?" Reed chuckled.

"Right here, dude." Theron laughed. "Lay it on us. What's your mate up to that's stressing you out?"

"Is it pregnancy?" Connor asked with a wince. "Pregnancy is hell. Tally is either eating, sleeping, or crying."

"What do you expect?" Ky laughed. "She's having twins."

"She's also having my balls for dinner if I tell her to relax," Theron growled.

"I learned you never tell a woman to take it easy," Gray told them, a look of knowledge on his face. "Lyss is also pregnant again, and when I suggested she take a nap and take it easy, that I'd watch our daughter, she argued with me until she fell asleep while denying she needed a nap."

"Nita isn't like that," Ky laughed. "She'll happily leave me with the kids and go to the spa. She says her only worry is that I'll let them play too rough and someone will be bleeding by the time she comes home."

"Maya is pretty good about resting now that we're having a baby. She lets me help around the house," Noah said with a grin and a waggle of his brows.

Theron and Connor looked at each other and laughed. "*Lets* you help?"

"I've yet to meet a woman who doesn't like a man who will clean around the house," Gray said with a chuckle. "Lyss will happily let me do all the cleaning and cooking if I ask her." He laughed harder at his words. "More like she'll somehow manage to make me want to do it with the promise of sex."

"Ah, yes." Noah laughed. "That's my reward for helping around the house, too."

"Us, too," Theron and Connor laughed.

"Wow," Ky said and lifted his drink. "Sex in exchange for housework."

"Here, here!" the group yelled.

"Now," Noah laughed and met Reed's gaze, "what did you do to get in the dog house?"

"Nothing."

"Mistake numero uno." Connor laughed. "Nothing is always something."

"Auri and I sort of had a break a while back. Five years ago, actually." He sat and took a sip of his beer. "She dumped me because I wasn't willing to have children."

The room became instantly silent.

"Why wouldn't you want offspring?" Gray asked.

"My mother left my father when I was a little kid. I had too many stepmoms who didn't give a shit about me, but loved my dad's money," he replied with enough bitterness in his words he heard it. "I had gotten into the mindset I wouldn't have kids and put them in the same situation."

"But, Reed," Ky frowned, "it wouldn't be the same. This is your mate. The woman you want to spend your life with. Your children would be loved and wanted by both of you."

Reed nodded and scrubbed a hand over the back of his neck. "Yeah, I know that now. Back then, I worried about the idea of kids."

"What changed your mind?" Theron asked.

"Yeah. Something had to happen to make you reconsider," Connor added.

He thought about the years past and all that had happened. So much changed in Reed that he was a different person now. "My little brother Gavin."

Noah nodded. "I heard about that. I'm sorry about your father, by the way."

"Thanks. Now I just need to figure out how to make her listen. She refuses to be in the same room with me." Even though the chemistry was still there, alive and kicking, he wanted more than sex. He wanted her love.

They had been apart too many years. In those years, he learned all he needed was her. Gavin had given him more lessons than he could ever thank his little brother for.

"So you need her to talk to you and you don't want to be interrupted?" Gray scratched his chin.

"Our mates are better at this than we are," Theron said. Connor nodded "Maybe we should ask them for help."

"This will definitely liven up this party. The ladies love getting involved in others' lives." Noah laughed.

"You do realize, Gerri will kill us if his mate sheds a single tear," Ky added.

The men nodded and they all pulled out their cell phones to message their women. These were the kind of friends Reed needed in his life.

CHAPTER EIGHT

Auri marched to the indoor garden, leaving the crowds behind. Gerri had taken one look at her face and sent her outside for a breath of fresh air. She walked dazedly through the maze of flowers, her mind a complete mess.

She made a turn and walked into the center of the garden where a group of women lounged by the flowers. She knew most of them from visits to her bakery. On different daybeds, fluffy chairs, and chaises, they were reading their cell phones like they all got a message at the same time.

"Aurelis!" Tally Barca snapped her phone shut and yelled with excitement. "I had no idea you were here, but I should have guessed from the desserts."

Auri rushed over to hug a very pregnant Tally in a black gauzy dress that draped over her baby bump. "You look beautiful, Tally!"

"Get over here and give me a hug," Nita, Tally's cousin ordered. She wore a silver dress in a sexy fitted bodice that made her voluptuous curves look amazing.

"Aurelis, you look gorgeous," Maya grinned and stood to give her a hug. Also pregnant, she wore another gauzy dress in green. "I, on the other hand, look like a Christmas ornament."

Auri laughed at the comparison. "You do not. You are glowing and beautiful. All of you are." She noted all the phones had disappeared. "Where's Daniella?" she asked.

"She's on bed rest," Lyss replied to which Tally nodded.

"Yes," Tally added, "her baby's due any day and Kane and Blake didn't want to take any chances.

She nodded. Everyone was having babies, except her. She was happy for her friends and sad for herself.

"Oh, honey, why that frown?" Nita asked. "Everything okay?"

She glanced from woman to woman. All shifters like her. She didn't need to lie. They all knew she was mated by now. Maybe not back when they'd been human, but now they could scent it. And they could definitely scent Reed all over her dress, like she could.

"You can talk to us," Maya patted an empty seat next to her on the side of the daybed. "Come, sit and chat."

"Yes. We'll help you however we can," Lyss said.

"I…" she cleared her throat. "I've been mated to a man who's been out of my life for five years. He recently showed up and decided he wants me back."

She didn't need to go on to see the anger on the other women's faces or the way they shook their heads.

"Why did he leave?" Tally asked.

"I told him I couldn't be with someone who didn't want children. That's my one wish. To have a big family," she replied. Nita nodded sympathetically. "When he said he didn't want kids and it wasn't up for debate, it broke my heart."

"That jerk!" Lyss growled. "How dare he wait to tell you and then say *it wasn't up for debate*. Did he at least give you a reason why he didn't want kids?"

She shook her head, feeling emptier with each word she spoke. "He didn't say much. Oh, he did state he hated the holidays and he'd never celebrate them either."

Maya gasped. "What a scrooge!"

"Yes!" Nita curled her lip in contempt. "He's not sounding like someone who deserves you, Aurelis."

"But you love him," Tally said with a sad turn of her lips. "Don't you?"

She nodded. "I don't know what to do. He's here and he's making my body crazy," she growled. "I want to send him to hell but I want to know what's changed. Why he suddenly thinks I'm going to give him a chance." She sighed and let her shoulders slump. "More than that, I want to know why it took him five fucking years to come and talk to me."

"Oh, honey," Maya said and curled an arm around her, patting her shoulder. "You need to have it out with him."

Auri took a deep breath and let it out slowly. "This is not the place nor the time."

"Screw the place or time," Nita grumbled. "He has a lot of explaining to do."

"I agree with Nita," Lyss said. "I'd want to know now."

Tally nodded. "Where is this lovely male specimen?"

Auri laughed at the scheming look on Tally's face. "Somewhere inside. Probably trying to find me."

"Then let's go," Tally said, waddling to her feet. "I planned on spending the night sitting here, but this sounds more fun."

Maya nodded as she groaned to her feet with Auri's help. "Yeah, me too. Fixing your love life is definitely the highlight of this night."

Oh, joy.

CHAPTER NINE

Auri and the women entered the mansion through one of the doors close to the children's wing. She stopped at one of the entrances, flanked by the other women and gasped at what she saw.

"Aw," Maya said, "Look at that guy on the floor, playing with his little boy. Isn't it sweet?" Auri was too shocked to tell them Gavin was his brother. But did it matter?

"Yeah," Nita sighed. "Reminds me of Ky with our kids. He loves playing with them. A man who pays attention to his kids and gets down on their level is so precious."

"Aurelis?" Tally said her name softly and prodded her on the side.

Auri could barely move. That was Reed. But not the Reed she knew. This man truly enjoyed playing with Gavin. He chatted with him, and they put blocks together.

"I'm guessing this is the jerk?" Lyss giggled. "He doesn't look like a jerk from this angle."

"No way can he be a jerk when he's looking at that little boy with so much love," Maya stated with conviction Auri would have found humorous at another time. "Oh, look. The little guy is giving him a hug." Maya sniffled. "Damn, hormones. I cry at freaking car commercials."

Tally laughed and sniffled as well. "Auri, there has to be some mistake. I can tell from looking at him that he loves kids."

Auri shook her head. What the hell happened? Was she in a Twilight Zone episode? "I don't get it. He's acting the total opposite from what he told me when we were together."

"I hate to say this," Nita said, "but could he have changed in the time you were apart?"

"Five years is a long time," Lyss added. "Things happen to people."

"Maybe you should find a spot and have a chat with him," Maya suggested.

"What about one of the suites?" Tally asked.

"Gerri told me she had suites on the second level if any of us felt tired, we could use them."

"Yes, come on." Nita pulled her by the hand. "We'll send him your way and you can have a heart to heart."

Auri followed them in silence. Reed didn't want children. So why was he showing so much affection to Gavin. More than just brotherly love. He was making an effort at being a father figure and she needed to know why.

The walk to the suite was short since there was an actual elevator for the guests. With the mansion having five levels, someone had been smart enough to realize old knees didn't do steps well.

Once she was in the suite, she sat by the bed and recalled their last conversation before they'd broken up.

"I don't want kids. Ever."

Her heart felt torn from her chest. "What?"

"It's not up for discussion," he'd growled.

"Are you fucking crazy? You can't tell me that now. Children are a priority in my life. I want some and if you won't give them to me then I'm finding someone who will."

"You're mine, Auri. Don't ever forget it."

"I will not be any man's mate who refuses to have children. Send me divorce papers. We're through."

She'd been bluffing. Thinking maybe he'd give it some time and come back to talk to her, but he hadn't. He'd gone away and never looked back. Until now.

CHAPTER TEN

Reed was looking for Auri when he was surrounded by women.

"You're Reed Stone, right?" asked a very pregnant woman with an impish grin, in a black dress.

"I am."

She nodded. "We have a message for you, bub."

He raised his brows in surprise. "Okay."

"Aurelis told us to tell you she's in the purple suite waiting to speak with you."

He nodded and turned to go, but realized he was still surrounded by expectant faces.

"I know it's not any of our business, but do you love her?"

"Excuse me?"

"Sorry, I'm Maya. And I asked if you love her." She worried her bottom lip and then sighed. "If you don't love her, let her go, but if you do, you really need to open up."

"Hi, I'm Tally," said the one in the black dress. "And Maya's right. Children are a big deal to most women. Not all, but a lot of us. You knew she wanted babies and you waited to tell her how you felt..."

"But we've seen you with kids and we know you don't really mean that," said another. "Sorry, I'm Nita. Anyway, you must want kids now, right?"

He grinned at the last one who hadn't said anything and waited for her to speak.

"Hi, I'm Alyssa. Lyss. You know, if you love her, anything can be worked out. The most important part is honesty and communication."

He had to hand it to the men. Now that he met the men's mates, he realized what a handful the women had to be. They spoke their minds and came to the aid of a friend without holding back. They reminded him of Auri.

"Ladies, thank you for your advice, but I assure you that: One--I love Auri more than my own life. Two--I want children. All the children in the world she wants. And Three--I plan on being one hundred percent honest with her."

The women smiled and nodded. They made a space for him to leave.

"Good luck," they said in unison as they waved him away.

Yeah. He was going to need it.

CHAPTER ELEVEN

Auri glanced out the large window at the snowy forest. Christmas was her favorite time of year. Every season she was flooded with memories of things she did with her mom as a kid.

Trimming the tree and baking sugar cookies. Making traditional Latin foods like pastéles, roasted pork, and her dad's favorite, coquito. The spiked eggnog was a favorite among her family. She also remembered the chats with her mom and the walks to the park where they made snowmen. Lying on the fluffy snow and making snow angels. Not a single one of her favorite memories had anything to do with gifts, though those had been fun too. It was about family, friendships, and connecting with loved ones. That's why she loved the holidays.

The sound of the door opening had her turning.

"Should I stand here ready to dodge something or are you ready to listen to me?" Reed asked. That damn man and his casual way of ordering her around triggered her temper faster than a customer saying her cupcakes didn't have enough icing. She was trying to make the mini cakes healthier, geesh.

"That depends on what it is you need to tell me." She folded her arms over her chest and leaned on the window.

He took a few steps toward her and stopped. He hesitated, as if unsure what to do or say, then moved to sit on the bench at the foot of the massive bed. "I was wrong."

She snorted. "That's something I already know."

He frowned, his eyes glowing liquid gold. Oh, did he expect her to just sit quietly and allow him to have his say without giving her opinion? Too fucking bad. She was still angry over how things had gone down and there was no holding her tongue any longer.

"Just listen," he said softly. "When you told me you wanted children, I was dead set against it, but I was selfish." He met her gaze. "Yes, selfish. I didn't want to lose you over that."

"You knew how I felt about kids from the very beginning. It was the first thing we spoke of on our first date," she argued, unfolding her arms and curling her hands at her sides.

"I know," he growled. "I was an asshole. I wanted you all to myself and I didn't consider children that important."

"That's not all," she said. "You refused to spend any time with my family for our holiday gathering." She stood straight and glared at him. "Why? You didn't even know them and you wouldn't waste your time trying."

He growled and jumped to his feet. "You don't understand!"

"Then make me, because right now all I see is a selfish prick who—"

"My mother abandoned us just before Christmas when I was a little kid. Six years old." He turned and paced between the door and bed.

Her heart hammered hard in her chest as she listened to his words. "What?"

"We had the house set up. Everything was

decorated. She loved Christmas. She would send the cook away and bake and do all the awesome things kids want their moms to do." He met her gaze. Anger flashed through his eyes. "That wasn't enough for her. I wasn't enough. She left and not only did she not take me with her, she refused to acknowledge me as her son."

"How do you know? What if something happened—"

He silenced her with a deathly growl. "She decided she couldn't live with my father any longer. They weren't destined mates. They were just two people who married so they could make a pack strong. My father was a whiz at finances. He made everyone rich. But he also decided that if he met someone he wanted to sleep with, he would. Married or not." Reed ran his fingers through his short hair. "She chose that Christmas to get out. And left me behind."

"Did you ever search for her?"

He nodded. "When I was a teenager. She told me I wasn't her son, and she never wanted to see me again."

Her eyes grew wide with shock. "Oh, my god."

"I met Gerri around the same time. My dad was friends with her husband. They mentored me. I refused to speak to my father. I blamed him for my mother leaving. I blamed her for not caring. I blamed myself for not being good enough for her to love."

"Oh, Reed!" She darted to his side. "Don't say that. She made a bad choice. The worst choice, but that wasn't your fault." She pulled him to sit on the bench.

He continued. "Gerri talked to me. For a long time, I'd sit on her couch and try to decide what to do with myself." He glanced down and she did too. She didn't realize she'd grabbed his hand in hers. Dammit. There went staying angry. This meant nothing. He still had a lot of explaining to do.

"What did you come up with?" she asked.

"I decided I wouldn't have kids. I never wanted them to suffer what I did. I hated the holidays after that. Everything reminded me of her. Of how lonely I felt after she left. Alone and unwanted."

Christ. That was really hard to argue against. "Still, you could have told me all this. You had the time when we were getting to know each other those first few days."

He nodded. "I did. I was just more interested in getting to know your body better. I knew you were the woman I had been waiting for, but the vow I made myself didn't go away."

"So you waited until after you had me tied to you to tell me?" She started to get incensed again over his actions.

"I did. I know it was wrong. I didn't want to lose you. That's the real reason."

She nodded and pulled her hand from his. "Yeah, well you lost me anyway."

He grasped her hand and held tightly. "Don't say that." He gave her a desperate look. "I've changed. Things changed."

"How?"

"Gavin. He's made me see how much love there can be between a man and a baby. Even one that isn't yours."

"Explain," she ordered. "What exactly did Gavin do?"

"The first few weeks after you told me to leave, my father got a call after he'd remarried Rosemary." He sighed. "Unlike his previous marriages, this time it appeared they actually cared for each other."

"So where does Gavin come into play?"

"The call my father got was from a woman he'd slept with at some point between wives. She said she was pregnant and giving up the baby for adoption. That she'd rather the child go to a good family than give him to Charles, the womanizer." He gave a bitter laugh. "Seems she knew him pretty well."

"That was Gavin? The baby she was pregnant with?"

"Yes. I searched high and low; traveled everywhere to find her. I kept wanting to go back to you, but then my father got sick and all he asked was for me to find my brother." He let go of her hand and twined his fingers over his legs. "I swore I'd go back and talk to you, try to change your mind about kids, but then I found the woman. She'd already put Gavin up for adoption."

"Oh, no." She bit her lip. Poor little Gavin.

He nodded. "Yeah. I started to think it was for the best. The kid would have a good home and parents who cared about him. He wouldn't go through the shit I had, but my father wanted none of it. This was his son, and he had to be part of our family."

She turned to face him better, watching different emotions play over his features. "You obviously found him."

He smiled. A genuine love-filled smile. "I did. He was still a baby, only months old, living in an orphanage full of kids. Too many kids with no families or anyone to love them. I knew how they felt even though I had a custodial parent. It tore me apart to see so many of them."

He rubbed his hands on his knees. "I remember the first time I picked up Gavin and held him." He laughed; his face lit up with the memory. "He gave me a toothless smile and drooled on my suit."

She smiled, loving how much that moment appeared to have impacted him. "He's a great little boy."

"He is. I realized my father was right. He needed to be with our family, needed to know someone loved him. Someone cared." He pinned her with his gaze. "So I took over as his parent figure. Rosemary has been amazing with him, but he really looks up to me for everything." He lifted a hand to her face, caressing her jaw. "I realize now that any child we have would be immensely loved by not just me, but you too. There wouldn't be any feelings of being alone or forgotten."

She licked her lips, her emotions battling themselves over what she wanted. Sure, she wanted him and now that he appeared to know the love of a child he was changed, but how much?

He leaned in and pressed his lips to hers, kissing her softly and heating her blood. She gave in. *Only this one time.* She knew that was the biggest lie she'd told herself. His tongue probed her mouth. Stroking. Tasting. Taking.

She gripped at his tux jacket, shoving the material off his body, wanting to feel his skin. The jacket came off and he tugged on the bodice of her dress. Cool air puckered her nipples tightly.

His hands came up to her tits. He cupped and circled her engorged nipples with his thumbs. A pleasant warmth started at the pit of her belly and spread outward through her limbs.

He lowered his head to her chest, licking and suckling from one nipple to the other. Her breaths came in low, achy moans. She gripped his shirt, aware that if she let her own animal loose, the material would be shredded in no time. There was no guarantee that wasn't about to happen.

He lifted the gauzy fabric of her skirt to her waist, pressing a hand between her spread large thighs and feeling the wetness at the her center. She wanted him. Oh, how she wanted him. There was no denying it. Ever.

"Ah, babe," he grunted, lowering to the floor and pushing her knees apart farther. "The scent of your arousal makes me so fucking hard I can come from just looking at how wet you are."

She tilted her hips and leaned back, putting the

weight of her upper body on her elbows. She gripped the soft, cotton bedspread and moaned as his fingers pushed her wet underwear to the side and delved into her heat. "Reed…"

"Not once in the past five years have I forgotten how good you smell," he said, brushing his nose over her sex. "Or how fucking delicious you taste." He swiped his tongue over her clit. She squirmed and wished she could see better, but her dress was in the way. She lay back on the bed, glancing at the gorgeous chandelier and intricate artwork on the ceiling but not paying attention to.

The sound of material tearing got her attention. She felt her panties coming off without being slid down her legs. So like Reed. He'd been the reason she'd bought so many pairs of underwear when they'd first met.

He curled his big arms around her thighs and draped them over his shoulders, hauling her ass off the bed. He feasted on her pussy, licking and groaning with every slide of his tongue on her folds.

"This," he said, slipping two digits into her channel, "is mine."

"God!" she whimpered. Her muscles tightened. The impending orgasm neared.

He slid his fingers out of her and back in, deeper. He hooked them and pulled, rubbing nerves that made her gasp. "You," he growled, "are mine. Only mine. Always mine."

Fuck. Fuck. Fuck. She was so close. All she needed was another slide of his fingers and she'd be a goner. He did better than that. He sucked her clit between his lips, nibbling on the bit of flesh that held the secrets to her universe, and sent her soaring.

Her pussy clenched his fingers and a loud, moan left her lips. The sheets she'd been holding tore with the strength of her pull. Her body shook with every continued contraction and mini orgasm that racked her to the core.

He pulled her up and kissed her. She tasted herself on his lips. It was sexy and dirty and it turned her on so much. He guided her to the bench they'd been sitting on and motioned for her to kneel with her back to him. She did as he asked and his arms wrapped around her, bending her forward. He stepped back and draped the bottom of her dress over her waist.

"You are and will always be the most beautiful woman I have ever laid eyes on."

She wiggled her ass and felt his hands spread

her cheeks. Then a kiss landed on the crack then a slow glide of his tongue down to her hot entrance.

"Reed," she mumbled, her lungs burning with the need for air.

The sound of his zipper echoed along with their breathing in the large room. Then he was there, pressing the head of his cock into her. Filling her.

"That's it," he said when she pushed into him, taking all of him. "Let your body suck my dick." He gripped her hips and propelled back. "It's time to fill your tight little pussy with my cum. Time to fill you with my seed. To get my woman full with my child." He pushed forward hard, making her grip the edge of the bed. "Time to give you that baby we both want."

Aw, hell. He said he wanted one too. There was something so erotic about knowing the man she had fallen helplessly in love with wanted her for himself and to be the mother of his children.

She glanced over her shoulder at him and saw the look of pure, wild hunger in his eyes. The animal she knew so well lay right below the surface and he wanted out. He wanted her.

"Hurry, Reed," she urged. Her muscles started

to tighten and tension wound around her belly like a snake.

"I've got you, baby." He caged her with one arm at her side, still fucking her mercilessly. Harder and harder. Faster and deeper. He licked the back of her right shoulder and a shudder raced down her spine. He'd licked the same spot when he'd mated her. Back when he'd claimed her as his.

"What are you doing," she breathed out. "Reed, you can't—"

"You're mine," he growled. "It's time to remind you of that." He curled the hand he had on her hip around her waist and between her pussy folds, pressing at her clit. She gasped, choking on a scream. Her body unraveled, pleasure darting through her body, every cell dancing with joy.

He bit down. He embed his canines into her shoulder and came hard, filling her with his cum. A loud growl sounded from where he had her flesh clenched between his teeth. The vibrations from his body shook hers and sent a new wave of pleasure riding through her.

Her pussy sucked it all in. Her body took his seed, every drop that filled her, cooled the fire in her sex. He came for long moments, until she could feel his cum leaking from her pussy and down her legs.

"Stay there," he said, placing kisses on the bite area and pulling out of her body.

As if she could move. She was half on/half off the bed and her legs shook beneath her. He was back moments later with a warm hand towel, wiping her clean.

She had no idea what the heck she was going to do now, but one thing was for sure, they couldn't go back to the way things were.

CHAPTER THIRTEEN

She glanced at the falling snow and sighed. Her family invited her to a Christmas Eve celebration at cousin Violet's house. They'd drink coquito and eat pastéles and do all the awesome things she loved that made her family wonderful. But her heart wasn't in it.

She had left the party after telling Reed she needed some time to think about what to do. He couldn't just return and expect her to forgive him like nothing had happened. Like he hadn't hurt her. She didn't work like that.

At least he'd been understanding and though he looked ready to argue, he'd nodded and let her go. That had been three days ago. She still didn't know what to do. On one hand, she was happy Reed had gotten over his baby issues and learned to love children thanks to Gavin. But on the other hand, she was worried he'd come back with the whole scrooge thing and hurt her feelings again.

The bell dinged as people entered her bakery. She knew the ladies well.

"Tally and Lyss." She laughed. "Shouldn't you two be resting or something?"

Tally raised a brow and Lyss scrunched her nose. "You must be confusing us for people who don't have stuff to do."

She shook her head and took out a tray of chocolate chip cookies, blondies, and miniature napoleons. "Here, have at 'em."

Tally and Lyss waddled to the tray and grabbed up treats. "Not that we are here for this," Tally started, then laughed.

"We are totally here for this." Lyss grinned between bites.

"Okay, we are here for this and to take you somewhere." Tally picked up a chocolate chip cookie and sighed. "Say yes, and let's go."

Lyss gave Tally an alarmed look. "Can we take the cookies?"

They turned to Auri and she burst into giggles. "Yes. By all means don't let me keep two pregnant women from cookies. I might find myself being hurt."

"Maybe a little," Tally agreed.

"Okay. Let me close up and we can go." She'd only opened to send out orders people had placed in advance. Now she could leave.

———

"CLOSE YOUR EYES," Tally ordered. "You can open them once we're inside the gates."

Auri wanted to say this was silly, but she did as asked and closed her eyes for a few minutes. Last thing she'd seen was a private road and lots of forest.

"What is this place?" Auri asked when she was allowed to open her eyes. They arrived at a big building in the middle of the countryside. She'd missed the front entrance and the name of the place. It looked like a five star resort in the woods.

"You'll see," Tally said, tugging her along. For a pregnant woman with twins, she had some serious strength and stamina.

"Hey!" Nita waved from one of the side entrances. "This way."

"This is getting all kinds of weird," Auri told

them.

"Relax," Lyss said. "Our dark side has cookies. You made them, remember?"

Auri laughed and followed. They went into the clearly newly remodeled building and walked down a hallway where Maya waved them forth. "Oh, great. You're here. Come on."

Auri had no idea what was going on at that point, but she continued after the women. They got inside a room and someone sprayed something around her.

"Is that hunter's block?" she asked, recognizing the spray hunters used when they didn't want animals to smell the human scent.

"Yes. You need it. Just go with me on this," Maya winked.

"So is everyone here?" Gerri asked, entering the room.

Auri should have known Gerri was behind this. "Seems we're all here," she replied. "What are you up to, Gerri?"

Gerri shrugged her shoulders innocently. "I've no idea what you're talking about, Aurelis, but come on. There is something we want you to see."

Great. Nobody wanted to give her a clue but she had a feeling whatever it was, it was important.

Reed shoved his hand under the big white beard and scratched. The damn thing was annoying and hot. He wanted to get out of the costume, but the smiles on all the kids' faces were priceless.

He HO-HO-HO'd his way into the large room decorated with handmade ornaments and paintings made by the children in Gavin's Home, an orphanage for children who had been abandoned by their parents. The older kids had set up a huge tree with the help of the staff, and the younger ones made finger paintings and art to decorate the walls.

The big thing about Gavin's Home was Reed bought the building when he found his brother.

Ever since, he'd seen all those children needing more care and someone who really wanted to love them, he opened the place, hired a staff of amazing people and made sure every child felt they had someone who cared.

Right at that moment, his role as Santa was greeted by a bunch of screaming children happy to see him, including his own baby brother, Gavin.

He sat on the big chair the kids labeled with "Santa" and patiently called each child up by name. It had taken him a few days to put names with faces, but now it paid off when he could speak to a kid and be able to hold a conversation about what they truly liked and their hopes and dreams.

One of the bigger kids, a boy going on eight came up to him and shook his hand. Dylan. Reed was always amused by the business-like manner on the boy.

"Hello, Dylan."

"Hi, Santa." Dylan grinned. "Thank you for coming. I wasn't sure if you got my letter."

"I did get your letter. You mentioned your request wasn't one you wanted to put into writing and I wanted to ask you what it is so we can make it happen."

Dylan plopped on a chair next to Reed and

glanced up at him. The little boy's eyes were filled with hope. "I want a gift, but I don't want it for myself."

Like some of the other kids at Gavin's Home, Dylan probably wanted to ask for something one of the others didn't dare request. Reed was used to it. He was always amazed at how selfless the children were.

"Okay. I will do my best to help you out."

"It's about Gavin's brother, Reed," Dylan said quietly.

Reed raised his brows in surprise. He hadn't seen that coming. "What about him?"

"I heard someone say he was married but he looks really sad all the time." Dylan glanced at him with confusion. "Do you think his wife is upset he spends so much time here?"

Fuck. He really hadn't seen that coming. "No. I assure you Reed's wife loves children. She is one of the most giving and caring people in the world. I'll bet you one of these days she'll come visit you all."

Dylan's eyes lit up with happiness. "You really think so? I don't want Reed to get in trouble for coming to be with us. We want him to be happy, too."

Reed sighed. "I know you do. Reed wants you

all to be very happy. And his wife wants the same thing."

"I'd like to meet her," Dylan piped up with a smile. "I'm sure she has to be really nice to be married to Reed. He's awesome."

Reed laughed and shook his head. "I don't know if Reed would consider himself awesome, but he definitely loves everyone in this place. And yes, she's very nice. Hopefully one day you will get to meet her."

CHAPTER FIFTEEN

Auri wiped at the tears rolling down her cheeks. She turned to look at the other women who were also dabbing at their eyes with tissue.

"Damn hormones," Tally grumbled.

"That's your excuse," Nita laughed, "what's mine?"

They all laughed and Auri glanced at Gerri. "I don't understand. What is this place?"

Gerri grinned with a twinkle bright in her blue eyes. "I think it's your turn to sit on Santa's lap."

She nodded. The idea that Reed wasn't the scrooge she'd thought him to be for so long confused her even more. She walked around the back of the giant tree they'd been standing behind and headed for Santa. She saw the moment he glanced at her. He sat straighter on the chair, as if wanting to stand and go to her.

One of the employees, dressed as an elf smiled and guided her to his chair. She pointed to the chair set up next to him, but Auri declined and went for his lap.

The kids laughed and clapped. She curled her arms around his neck and gazed into his eyes. "What in the world is going on here?"

"How did you get here?" he asked.

"That's beside the point. What is this place?" She glanced around, noticing the perfectly main-tained building and the children in their nice clean clothes.

"It's called Gavin's Home," he said. "After I found him, I realized there were so many children who didn't have someone to care for them or give them the love and attention they needed. So I came up with the idea to bring some of them here." He motioned to the back of the room with his head.

She glanced at the bigger kids taking turns playing and drawing with the smaller ones as staff watched and participated nearby.

"The older ones learn a trade and get scholar-ships. They each have a counselor and a mentor.

They all go to therapy to rid them of unwanted feelings."

"Oh my gosh," she gasped. "Do none of them ever get adopted?"

He nodded. "Some. The little ones have better luck with that, which is why I set up a lot of big kid adoptions too. Everyone wants to find a place to call home, but if they don't, this will be a good home for them too."

She cupped his face in her hands. "You've been doing this since we separated?"

"Yeah. It bothered me to find so many children feeling neglected when I found Gavin. This was my way to help."

"You do realize you're dressed as Santa, right?" She blinked. "I thought you didn't do Christmas."

He shrugged. "People change. I did. As long as it makes one of these kids smile, I will dress up as whatever they want."

That was the moment her heart let go of the uncertainty and she knew giving him and their relationship another chance was the right move.

"You know something," she leaned in to whisper to his ear. "I have a single wish from Santa this year."

His eyes twinkled with heat. "What's that?"

"I don't know if I'll get it."

He laughed. "Have you been a naughty girl?"

She shrugged. "Not yet. But I plan on it."

"What do you want, love?"

"You. Us. I love you, Reed," she whispered and pressed her lips to his, ignoring the fake beard and the giggling children.

He hugged her tightly and kissed her back. Behind them they heard applause and they separated to look over her shoulder. Tally and her mates, Nita and Ky, Lyss, and Gray and Maya and Noah all smiled with Gerri in front lifting a glass of grape juice. "To love children," she said, "is to live."

"Auri," Reed said, taking her attention back to his face. "I really do want children. I want all the kids you want, baby," he told her. "I want Christmas together, with our friends, family, hell, with whomever you want, just as long as I have you."

She smiled wide at the way he sounded so committed to making her wishes come true. "I like your proposition so far." She laughed at the image of him as scrooge now that she saw him dressed as Santa. "I can't believe I used to think of you as scrooge."

He leaned into her ear. "I'll show you scrooge. I'll scrooge the hell out of you when I get you home."

She giggled hard, loving the bad pun. "Oh, please do. Please, scrooge me hard."

He laughed right along with her and pressed a kiss to her lips. "I plan to."

She didn't bother turning around to look at their friends' faces when they heard them snickering over what they'd said. Those shifters and their super hearing.

Gerri sat back on the plush seat at Aurelis's bakery and glanced at the tray of cookies and tea in front of her.

"Anything else I can get you?" Violet, Auri's cousin asked.

She was minding the bakery while Auri and Reed had a mini honeymoon.

"I'm great, darling."

"So how's your new assistant working out?" Violet asked Gerri.

"Pretty great, actually. Which is why I don't think it will last," she sighed.

Violet grinned. "That doesn't make sense. If she's so great, why wouldn't she last?"

"One of these blasted shifters will take her after all my hard work at training her. I just know it."

"I'm sorry," Violet said sympathetically.

"Oh, no, darling. I'm not angry about it. I love matching people, but I hate having to retrain assistants."

"I think you need some real chocolate if you're thinking about training anyone," Violet said and went off. Gerri watched her get a piece of cake. She wondered if Violet might be interested in her services. It was time to get to know Auri's cousin better.

THE END…for now!

New York Times and USA Today Bestselling Author

Hi! I'm Milly Taiden. I love to write sexy stories featuring fun, sassy heroines with curves and growly alpha males with fur. My books are a great way to satisfy your craving for paranormal romance with action, humor, suspense and happily ever afters.

I live in Florida with my hubby, our son, and our fur babies: Speedy, Stormy and Teddy. I have a serious addiction to chocolate and cake.

I love to meet new readers, so come sign up for my newsletter and check out my Facebook page. We always have lots of fun stuff going on there.

SIGN UP FOR MILLY'S NEWSLETTER FOR LATEST NEWS!

http://eepurl.com/pt9q1

Find out more about Milly Taiden here:

Email: millytaiden@gmail.com

Website: http://www.millytaiden.com

Facebook: http://www.facebook.com/millytaidenpage

Twitter: https://www.twitter.com/millytaiden

Nightflame Dragons

Dragons' Jewel *Book One*

Dragons' Savior *Book Two*

Dragons' Bounty *Book Three*

Dragon's Prize *Book Four*

Wintervale Packs

Their Rising Sun *Book One*

Their Perfect Storm *Book Two*

Their Wild Sea *Book Three*

A.L.F.A Series

Elemental Mating *Book One*

Mating Needs *Book Two*

Dangerous Mating *Book Three*

Fearless Mating *Book Four*

Savage Shifters

Savage Bite *Book One*

Savage Kiss *Book Two*

Savage Hunger *Book Three*

Savage Caress *Book Four*

Drachen Mates

Bound in Flames *Book One*

Bound in Darkness *Book Two*

Bound in Eternity *Book Three*

Bound in Ashes *Book Four*

Federal Paranormal Unit

Wolf Protector *Federal Paranormal Unit Book One*

Dangerous Protector *Federal Paranormal Unit Book Two*

Unwanted Protector *Federal Paranormal Unit Book Three*

Deadly Protector *Federal Paranormal Unit Book Four*

Paranormal Dating Agency

Twice the Growl *Book One*

Geek Bearing Gifts *Book Two*

The Purrfect Match *Book Three*

Curves 'Em Right *Book Four*

Tall, Dark and Panther *Book Five*

The Alion King *Book Six*

There's Snow Escape *Book Seven*

Scaling Her Dragon *Book Eight*

In the Roar *Book Nine*

Scrooge Me Hard *Short One*

Bearfoot and Pregnant *Book Ten*

All Kitten Aside *Book Eleven*

Oh My Roared *Book Twelve*

Piece of Tail *Book Thirteen*

Kiss My Asteroid *Book Fourteen*

Scrooge Me Again *Short Two*

Born with a Silver Moon *Book Fifteen*

Sun in the Oven *Book Sixteen*

Between Ice and Frost *Book Seventeen*

Scrooge Me Again *Book Eighteen*

Winter Takes All *Book Nineteen*

You're Lion to Me *Book Twenty*

Lion on the Job *Book Twenty-One*

Beasts of Both Worlds *Book Twenty-Two*

Bear in Mind *Book Twenty-Three*

Bring to Bear *Book Twenty-Four*

Dragon Rights *Book Twenty-Five*

Wolfing Her Down *Book Twenty-Six*

Also, check out the **Paranormal Dating Agency World on Amazon**

Or visit http://mtworldspress.com

The Alien Warrior's Woman *Book One*

The Alien's Rebel *Book Two*

Contemporary Works by Milly Taiden

Mr. Buff

Stranded Temptation

Lucky Chase

Their Second Chance

Club Duo Boxed Set

A Hero's Pride

A Hero Scarred

A Hero for Sale

Wounded Soldiers Set

If you enjoyed the book, please consider leaving a review, even if it's only a line or two; it would make all the difference and would be very much appreciated.

Thank you!